W9-AHG-969

A Roomful of Questions

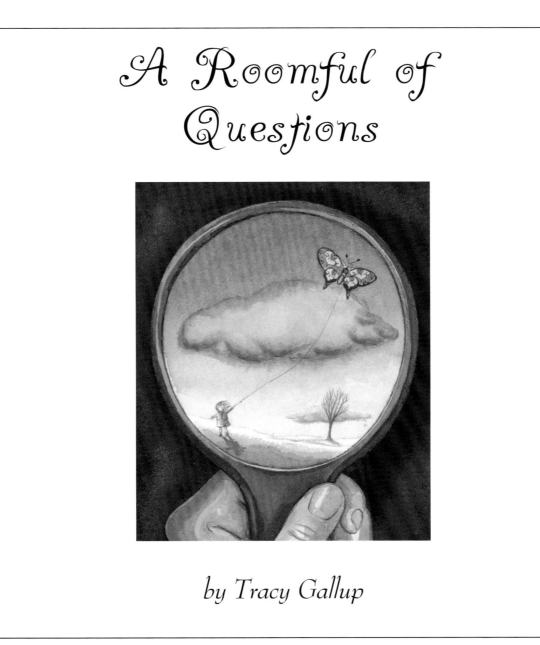

by Tracy Gallup

For Doug, who encouraged me to dream in black and white.

"…be patient toward all that is unsolved in your heart and try to love the *questions themselves* like locked rooms and like books that are written in a very foreign tongue. Do not seek the answers…*Live* the questions now."

-Rainer Maria Rilke

Letters To A Young Poet, translation by M.D. Herter Norton

Who plants the seeds
in the garden of thought?

Do our dreams understand our secrets?

*Is there a song
that is mine alone?*

*Are tears the beginning
or the end of things?*

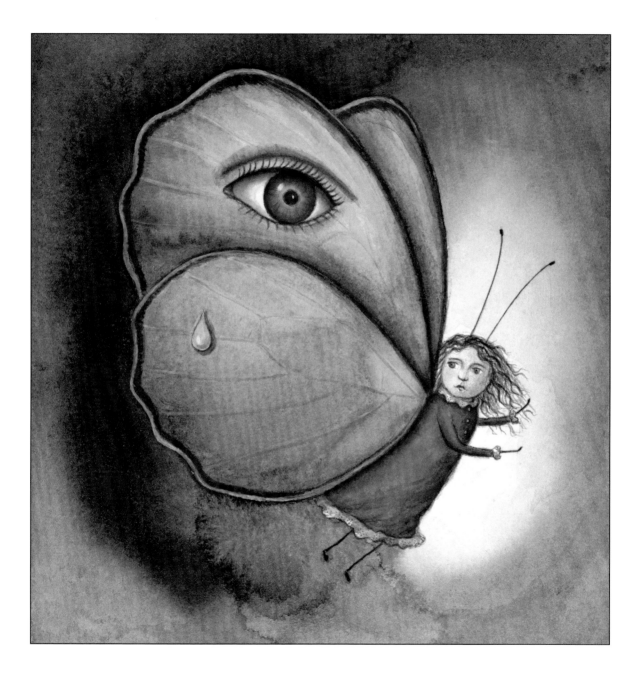

Is it the journey or the destination
that matters?

Is magic
in every one of us?

Where is the me
I was?

Is anything always?

If the earth is our home
can we ever be lost?

*Must we leave
to know what we have left?*

The universe and myself,
are we one?

What should we do
with the beauty we love?

Are things that never happened
true?

Who can I ask?

Copyright 2008 by Tracy Gallup

All rights reserved. No part of this book may be reproduced in any form or by any
electronic or mechanical means, including information storage and retrieval systems,
without express written permission from the publisher, except by a reviewer who may
quote brief passages in a review.

Library of Congress
Cataloging-in-Publication Data on file

Tracy Gallup
A Roomful of Questions
Art Direction by Tom Mills

ISBN 978-1-934133-44-6
Fiction

10 9 8 7 6 5 4 3 2 1

A Mackinac Island Press, Inc. publication
www.mackinacislandpress.com

Printed in Canada